# RESCUE RIDERS

## Race Against Time

*Also by Peter Clover*
*published by Hodder Children's Books*

# RESCUE RIDERS

## Race Against Time

## Peter Clover

Illustrations by Shelagh McNicholas

Hodder
Children's
Books

A division of Hodder Headline Limited

# For Stephen Blue and Missy – with love

Text copyright © 1998 Peter Clover
Illustrations copyright © 1998 Shelagh McNicholas

First published in Great Britain in 1998
by Hodder Children's Books
This edition published 2000

A Catalogue record for this book is available
from the British Library

ISBN 0 340 72679 2

Typeset by Hewer Text Ltd, Edinburgh
Printed and bound in Great Britain by Guernsey Press

Hodder Children's Books
a division of Hodder Headline Limited
338 Euston Road
London NW1 3BH

# One

I *will* ride this pony! thought Hannah. Today, she was more determined than ever. Hannah went riding every Saturday morning at the stables not far from her house. They had lots of ponies but, as usual, they had given her Pudding to ride. The pony's *real* name was Bracken but Hannah thought he looked more like a

1

Pudding. He was a fat dapple grey who dreamed along behind all the others.

'Come on!' yelled her friend Charlotte, who was ahead of her as they made their way down the quiet country lane. 'Kick him on!'

'You're not supposed to kick,' said Hannah. 'You're meant to squeeze with your calves.' She squeezed Pudding's fat sides with all her strength, but it made little difference. Pudding's slow amble didn't falter.

'You've got to let him know you mean business,' said Charlotte. She had pulled up her pony to wait for Hannah. 'You'll never make a rider if you don't take control, Han.'

Just then, Pudding shied suddenly at a ferocious paper bag rustling in the hedge and gave a little sideways hop. Hannah lost her balance and felt herself slipping but quickly pushed one heel down in her stirrup and pulled herself upright again.

'Phew! That was close,' she breathed.

Butterflies danced in her tummy as she tightened the reins.

Up ahead, at the front of the line, Mrs Bellows stood up in her stirrups and raised her arm in the air.

'Trot ON,' she yelled.

Charlotte kicked her pony on. The chestnut mount shot forward like a flying conker.

Hannah's legs flapped like sails and, without altering his stride, Pudding plodded stolidly on.

'Come along at the back there. UP down, UP down, UP down,' yelled Mrs Bellows. 'You're holding up the line, Hannah.' But it made no difference. Pudding would go at his own pace until they reached the bend in the lane which meant they were heading back to the stables. That was the bit Hannah liked best of all. There was no stopping Pudding then.

As everyone else slowed their ponies down to a walk, Pudding decided to put on a spurt. Head down and he was

off! Straight through the line he went, along the narrow lane at a fast lurch. Hannah bumped along clumsily in the saddle.

'Up down, up down, up down,' she chanted hopefully.

Charlotte laughed as her best friend headed down the lane, blonde ponytail bouncing, hanging on awkwardly as Pudding went straight through the gates and into the riding school.

As they unsaddled their ponies afterwards, Charlotte said, 'Next week you should ask for a different pony, Han. You'll never learn to ride properly if they keep giving you Bracken.'

Hannah knew that Charlotte was right, of course. But the truth was, she was still a little nervous of other ponies. Hannah liked Pudding because he *was* such a reliable plodder. It'll be different when I've got my *own* pony though, she thought. A pony I can really get used to. One day soon. *That* will surprise everyone. I'll be riding like the wind, then!

But she didn't tell Charlotte her plan just yet. She didn't tell her how she was going to save up all her pocket money to buy a pony of her very own. The pony of her dreams. A golden palomino with a creamy white mane. When he moved, his feet would barely touch the ground. He would almost seem to fly.

'I expect you're looking forward to going on holiday tomorrow,' said Charlotte suddenly, pulling off her riding hat and running a hand through her dark bobbed hair.

Hannah came down to earth with a bump.

'Arghh!' she groaned. She had forgotten all about that for a moment. 'A holiday with Frankenstein.' Hannah pulled a face.

Her mum's fiancé was called Frank. Hannah could hardly believe that he was going to become her new dad. Not that she'd ever known her real father –

he'd died when she was only a baby – but she'd got by this long without a dad and she wasn't sure she was ready for a new one now – *especially* not Frankenstein.

'Why do you call him Frankenstein?' smiled Charlotte.

'Because he's tall and his head is flat on top. He looks like Frankenstein's monster.'

'No, he doesn't,' said Charlotte as she hung up her pony's bridle. 'You know he doesn't. He's really handsome. You only

call him that because he's going to marry your mum and you're jealous!'

'No, I'm not!' snapped Hannah. 'Anyway, he's mean. He's got loads of money but he won't buy me a pony. He says I've got to save up for it myself. Well, at least half, anyway.'

Hannah hadn't meant to tell Charlotte about the pony yet but it just slipped out.

'A pony! You can't be having a pony,' said Charlotte.

'I am,' said Hannah. 'When I save up half, I'm going to have a palomino.'

'Wow,' said Charlotte. 'A palomino. Will you keep him here at the stables? Will you let me ride him?'

'You can ride him whenever you want,' said Hannah. 'Well,' she added, 'all the time I'm not riding him.'

As they stood by the riding-school gates, waiting for Charlotte's father to pick them up, Hannah talked about the holiday.

Frankenstein was a sporty type. A hairy-legged jogger from the Hartfield Harriers. He'd met Hannah's mum when she'd joined the running club to keep fit.

That was over a year ago now and since then the pair of them had joined step aerobics and the County Kayak Club too. This holiday was going to be an outward-bound adventure in a canoe. Fun for all the family, Frankenstein had said.

'Is Miles going?' asked Charlotte.

'Yes, we're all going.'

'He'll be your brother, you know,' said Charlotte. 'When your mum gets married to Frank. Your big bruv! Big bruvver Milo.'

Hannah pulled a face. 'I know,' she groaned.

'Till death do you part,' said Charlotte.

'It's not *me* that's getting married.' Hannah pretended to be cross. 'Marry Miles! Over my dead body.'

'Who'd want to marry *you* anyway,' laughed Charlotte. Hannah gave her a friendly push. 'Do you want to hear about this holiday or not?'

They were going to drive up to the Welsh mountains and canoe down a river through the open valleys and country-side. Mum and Frankenstein were taking the canoe, and Hannah and Frank's son, Miles, were to follow the course of the river along a bridle-path, riding pack ponies. They would be carrying all the supplies and equipment.

This trip of a lifetime would take five days with stops along the way. That was why Hannah was dreading it. Five whole days stuck up a mountain on a strange pony.

'It sounds fantastic,' said Charlotte. 'What an adventure! I wish I was going.'

'You can go instead of me if you like,' said Hannah quickly. 'You can marry Miles and I'll stay here and ride Pudding.'

Charlotte was still laughing as her father's

car crunched to a halt on the gravel outside Hannah's house. 'You are funny,
Han. And I want to hear all about it when
you get back!'

'Don't worry. You will,' moaned
Hannah.

# Two

The next day was the start of Hannah's holiday. The nightmare holiday, Hannah thought but didn't say. That would have upset her mum. And Hannah knew how much her mum had been looking forward to them all going away together. Instead, Hannah sat in the back of the car with a big pretend smile pasted across her face.

She glanced sideways at Miles. He was scribbling something in a notebook balanced on his knee. If she could have chosen, Hannah would have preferred a younger brother. Or better still an older sister. But she was stuck with Miles.

Miles was sixteen. And not very chatty. They'd been in the car for a full ten minutes and Miles hadn't said a word.

Hannah knew that Miles didn't talk to anyone much. But she noticed that he scribbled a lot in his silly notebooks. He was always doing it. The first time they had met he had barely managed to say hello. Getting Miles to talk was like drawing blood from a stone. Well, he can sit there in silence for all I care, thought Hannah. Charlotte would drag a conversation out of him but I can't be bothered. After all, like she'd told Charlotte, *she* wasn't marrying Miles, so it didn't matter.

Hannah leaned back into the seat, pulled her legs up and hugged her knees. She studied the back of Frank's head. It really was flat on the top. And he had such a big thick neck. She didn't care if he *was* handsome, he still reminded her of Frankenstein's monster.

Hannah was bored. She leaned forward as Frankenstein drove through the village.

'How long will it take to get there?' she asked.

'It's a good four-hour drive,' said Frank cheerfully. 'But don't worry, we'll be there in no time at all.'

He turned and smiled at Hannah's mum all lovey-dovey. Hannah hated the way her mum fluttered her eyelashes like that. She collapsed back heavily into the seat with a big sigh and blew her wispy blonde fringe out of her eyes.

'Where will we sleep?' asked Hannah. 'We don't have a tent or anything, do we?'

'Under the trees,' laughed Frank.

'*What?* We'll freeze to death!' Hannah shot forward again and poked her head in between the two front seats. 'There might be snakes, or wolves, or vampire bats!'

Miles chuckled to himself.

'I don't think so, Hannah,' said Mum. 'And stop teasing her, Frank. Everything's arranged. There's a base camp at the foot of the mountains, where we leave the car. A ranger will take us up to the mountain pass where the river starts. There, we pick the canoe up along with ponies for you two and make our way down river through the valley, stopping each evening at an outpost. Each site has log cabins by the river. We'll be cooking on a barbecue and sleeping in our own little woodland cabin. Won't that be fun, Hannah? Miles?'

Miles grunted and Hannah sat back again. Her head buzzed with questions. What sort of pony would she get? Would it be a plodder or really manic and wild? And would she be able to handle it?

Mum said it would be quite safe. The mountains were gentle and a bridle-path followed the river at an easy, winding pace. But Hannah was still nervous. It was all right for Mum and Frankenstein. They would be in a canoe. Easy-peasy. Riding the pack ponies was going to be the tricky part. She knew Miles could ride well. Hannah hoped she would be able to keep up. She glanced at Miles and they exchanged weak smiles.

The journey passed quite quickly. They only stopped once – to have a quick pub lunch – and by early afternoon they had reached base camp at the foot of their Welsh mountain. A sign hammered to a weathered post read *Llanstwyth Adventure Park*, in bold, green letters.

It looked less like a park than Hannah could ever have imagined. Flat, grey countryside stretched away in every direction as far as she could see, with only a few scraggy trees lining the mountain route ahead. The trees at home are taller and greener than these, thought Hannah.

'Here we are,' said Frankenstein. 'Out you both get.' He raced around the car and opened the passenger door for Hannah's mum.

Hannah let herself out and kicked at the loose gravel with the toe of her trainers.

Mum and Frank walked over to the small wooden lodge to register. Hannah moped about outside, imagining the wild stallion she was about to meet. I bet it's barmy and bonkers – or both, thought Hannah. She hoped that all her riding lessons were about to pay off. She didn't want to let everyone down. Or show herself up in front of Miles.

Hannah waved to Mum and Frank as they came out of the lodge.

'Are you coming now?' she called.

'Just going to park the car at the back, Hannah.'

When they reappeared, they were carrying four saddlebags packed with everything they would need for the trip. And holding hands. Yuck!

'Where's Miles?' asked Mum.

Miles was sitting under a tree. Hannah could see him. Head down, scribbling away in his notebook again.

'I'll fetch him,' chirped Hannah. She ambled across to Miles.

'They're waiting for us, Miles,' said Hannah, beaming her biggest smile and trying to sound friendly. Miles huffed an irritated sigh and snapped his notebook shut.

'Tell them I'm coming,' he said, without even looking at her.

Hannah frowned. 'Tell them yourself,' she said and flounced off. How un-friendly he was. She hoped he wasn't going to be a pain the *whole* holiday.

The park ranger bumped them all the way to the top of the mountain pass in the back of a dark-green Land Rover. There, cutting through a rocky plateau covered in low brush and scrub, was the start of the mountain river.

19

That wasn't quite as Hannah had imagined it either. No raging torrent of white-water rafting fame. No foaming waves, but a gentle bubbling course of crystal-clear river meandering into a forest of pine and mountain ash. But the view was magnificent. Hannah looked down the slope of the contoured hills across the tops of the trees. She saw the river glistening on its way through patches of woodland into the open valley and beyond. The sheer mountainside itself gleamed blue beneath the pale sky.

Frank put his arm around Hannah's shoulder.

'Well, Hannah, what do you think?'

'It's fantastic,' said Hannah. And she really meant it.

Mum gave her a big smile. 'I told you it was going to be special.'

Hannah looked at Miles and almost fell over. Miles was smiling too.

The ranger unlocked the door of a long, low wooden shed standing close to the

river. He went inside and dragged out a red, fibreglass canoe. It was so long, it just kept coming and coming as though he were unwinding it from a big reel somewhere inside. Finally the end came in sight.

The ranger dragged the canoe over to the bank and pushed it out into the river. He tied the mooring rope to a small wooden jetty, then went back inside for the paddles, helmets and life-jackets.

'Where are the ponies?' asked Hannah, the familiar butterflies starting to flutter in her tummy.

'They're coming,' said the ranger.

Then Hannah thought she heard something. A low whicker and the sound of hooves.

'Here they are!' said Mum.

Hannah sprang to attention as a young lad arrived on a pony, leading another by the rein. The boy slid from the saddle and tethered the ponies to a rail.

Hannah went up to the nearest pony

and walked around it. The pony was brown. Its coat was long and shaggy with a black mane and tail.

'There you are!' said Frank. 'A lovely chestnut pony, just for you.'

'It's not a chestnut,' said Miles. 'That colour's called dun!'

Mum smiled at Frank and raised her eyebrows.

'What's his name?' asked Hannah, stroking the pony's soft velvety muzzle. It didn't *look* barmy.

'He's called Flash,' said the lad.

I *knew* it, thought Hannah. *Flash*. He probably goes like supersonic lightning. The butterflies suddenly got worse.

She looked over at the other pony. It was bigger than Flash – about fourteen hands – and called Toffee because of its light caramel coat. Miles would be riding this one. Miles was already making friends and patting Toffee's glossy neck.

The ranger wished them all a good trip and climbed back into the Land Rover. The lad waved through the open window as they drove off, and then they were alone – with two ponies, the canoe, and the promise of adventure ahead.

# Three

Miles checked both ponies' girths and held the reins steady while Hannah mounted. Flash was a Welsh mountain pony and came with a guarantee that he was actually very slow, steady and perfectly reliable – just like Pudding. Hannah swung her leg easily over the pony's back and settled herself in the saddle. Then she took the reins loosely and let Flash nibble at a patch of dandelions with Toffee while Mum and Frank slipped on their life-jackets and climbed into the canoe.

Frank sat at the back and Mum sat in the front. With a smile and a wave they were off. The first outpost was only two hours away by river and it was still early afternoon, so there was no need to hurry. They could take things nice and easy.

Miles led the way on Toffee. Hannah kept her hands steady and waited until Flash stopped twisting about, then she squeezed with her heels and gently urged him forward.

Flash walked along happily behind Toffee as they followed the canoe along the bridle-path. The sun shone brightly overhead and, although Hannah still felt a little nervous, it was so brilliant to be riding out in the fresh mountain air that her nerves soon passed.

Mum and Frank handled the canoe expertly, and both were impressed with

Hannah as she rode steadily along keeping up with their progress.

Once or twice she lagged behind when Flash stopped suddenly for a snatch of grass. But Hannah's friendly voice in his ear soon encouraged him to keep going.

Hannah quickly gained confidence and even began to enjoy the ride. When the path suddenly levelled out into a nice flat stretch beneath a canopy of trees, she decided to try a trot.

Hannah shortened her reins and squeezed with her calves. Up down, up down, up down, just like Mrs Bellows had taught her. Flash responded brilliantly. Hannah found herself grinning broadly. The smile felt good on her face. She was really riding now. If only Charlotte and the others could see her.

Hannah could smell the river and hear the slap and drag of paddles in the water to her left.

'Ride him, cowgirl,' yelled Frank. Hannah was really chuffed. She felt her

face go red. Maybe Frankenstein wasn't so bad after all. And even Miles laughed when she passed him on Toffee at what felt like a hundred miles an hour and beamed him a bright smile.

Hannah noticed how happy her mum was, paddling the canoe with Frank, strands of hair escaping from under her helmet and blowing free in the breeze. She looked really pretty.

The bridle-path wound its way along, following the course of the river, in and out of the woodlands, never wandering too far from the riverbank. Hannah couldn't remember ever enjoying herself quite so much. She was really in control.

Hannah lengthened the reins and gave Flash his head. He seemed to know exactly what was expected of him and carried on with a steady stride.

Two hours passed very quickly, and soon the first camp came into sight. Out of the wooded valley, around a bend in the river, a little wooden cabin appeared.

Hannah could easily have carried on for another hour or so, but the log cabin meant they had reached their first stop.

Hannah rode Flash right up to the outpost and slid out of the saddle. She tethered the pony to a wooden rail on the cabin's covered veranda and skipped down to the river, while Miles secured Toffee.

Mum and Frank manoeuvred the canoe alongside a low wooden mooring platform and Frank threw the towline for Hannah to secure.

They climbed out on to the bank and Frank swept Hannah up in his strong arms.

'You were fantastic, Hannah.'

'And what about me?' said Mum, pretending to feel left out.

'You too, my angel. You were brilliant.'

Flash blew a loud snort and tossed his head.

'OK, *and* you, Flash. You were *all* magnificent.'

'I think he wants his supper,' laughed Mum.

There was a small tack room built on to the side of the cabin and a covered shelter for the ponies with a hay net and food bin. Frank offered to help with the saddles and bridles but Hannah wanted to do it all by herself. She even sent Miles away to scribble in his notebook.

'You two go inside and get everything ready,' said Hannah, 'and I'll look after Flash and Toffee.'

'OK, Captain,' teased Frank. He gave Hannah a salute and led Mum into the cabin with the saddlebags.

Hannah hung up the tack and settled Flash in. The first thing he wanted was a good drink. Hannah filled the water trough with fresh water from the outside tap and scooped pony mix from the food bin in the tack room into the feed mangers. Then she gave both ponies a quick rubdown and left them to feed while she went into the cabin.

Inside the cabin, the one main room was divided into both a sitting and a dining area. A long sofa stretched itself along one wall behind a low coffee table. There was a pine table with four upright chairs and a small kitchen with a gas cooker, a sink and a tiny cupboard storing cups, bowls, plates, saucepans, teapot and a kettle. In a single drawer beneath the cooker were knives, forks and spoons.

Two small bedrooms led off from the main living area. One had bunk beds, up against the wall. The other had a small single nestled in an alcove where the ceiling sloped down to meet the sides of the cabin.

Between the two bedrooms was a tiny bathroom. Miles had volunteered to sleep on the sofa. Fresh sheets and bedding were neatly folded on each bed. It was all very cosy, with little red gingham curtains everywhere and everything smelling of wood. Even the sheets smelled of pine.

Mum popped the kettle on while Frank lit a fire in the woodburner. It felt a little chilly inside.

While the kettle was boiling and Mum got the mugs and teapot out, Frank took Hannah outside to gather firewood from the forest. He wanted Miles to come too. But Miles had disappeared.

'It's just like *The Little House on the Prairie*,' said Hannah.

'Are you having a good time?' asked Frank. 'I hope so!'

Hannah smiled and nodded. She felt a little embarrassed, remembering how horrible she had been about Frank in the past.

They gathered enough firewood to last the night, then went back to the cabin for a steaming mug of hot tea and a digestive biscuit.

'We'll have a barbecue supper later,' said Frank. 'Real Boy Scout stuff.'

'What about us Brownies?' teased Hannah's mum, as she handed round the biscuits.

Frank laughed and gave her a playful shove.

They sat outside on the covered veranda, sipping tea and watching the river glide past their front door. A brown trout leaped clean out of the water. Birds twittered in the treetops above. It was magical.

Later that evening, Hannah tried to talk to Miles. He was sitting at the pine table with his notepad again, and masses of newspapers spread all around. Miles

was annoyed at being interrupted. Hannah was cheeky and said if he told her what he was writing, she would go away.

'I'm writing news,' said Miles. 'Well, not exactly *writing* news. I'm *re*-writing it. My way. Copying it out in my own words.' Miles wanted to be a newspaper reporter when he left school. A top journalist.

Hannah only half-understood what Miles was doing, but she knew that it was important to him, and left him in peace to go outside and check on the ponies.

Toffee blew a soft whicker when he saw Hannah. And Flash, being nosy, pushed his velvet muzzle into her hand, looking for a treat. She took a few pony nuts from the feed bin and palmed both ponies a titbit. Then Hannah stroked their necks and faces for a while before saying a final goodnight.

# Four

The next day was hot and muggy. They were all up bright and early. A quick breakfast on the veranda, then they packed everything up, ready to go. Frank and Miles tidied the cabin while Mum and Hannah washed all the dishes and cutlery and put them away. Then Hannah went out to tack up Flash.

He recognised Hannah immediately and began stomping his hooves in a little dance of greeting. Hannah stroked both ponies and planted a big kiss on Flash's nose. Flash blew a loud snort and cleared his nostrils. Then he began nudging Hannah's jacket pocket looking for a treat.

She put on the saddle and tightened the leather girth. Then she slipped on the bridle.

Miles came out to join her, tacked up, then strapped their two saddlebags in place. The stable lad would come in later to muck out and refresh the hay net and food bin.

Hannah was keen to get going. She had a longer ride ahead of her today. Frank said it was at least four hours to the next outpost. But they had all day and there was no need to race.

Hannah was looking forward to trying a canter if the bridle-path allowed it. She was hoping that Miles would give her some tips.

Frank and her mum wedged themselves into the canoe. Hannah thought the life-jacket made Mum look really fat. She laughed and blew out her cheeks at her as she waved them off.

The river was wider now but still meandered along at a gentle pace. The bridle-path followed the river out of the mountain forest and into the open valley. It was glorious, like a rocky range in a western movie. Sheep grazed on a distant slope. Welsh Blacks. The ranger had told Hannah to look out for them.

The bridle-path suddenly became very flat with a long stretch running ahead. Hannah hung back and let Mum and Frank get in front of her a little. Then she squeezed with her calves and gave Flash the command to canter.

The pony bounded forward with a smooth rolling motion. Hannah sat bolt upright with a straight back, pressing herself down into the saddle.

Unfaltering, Hannah took Flash at a

canter along the bridle-path. The sound of the pony's hooves thrilled Hannah to pieces. She had never been able to ride Pudding like this. Flash's stride felt easy and relaxed. She imagined she was riding like the wind on a golden palomino.

As she passed the canoe on her left, Mum called out with a cheer. Hannah was showing off and enjoying every minute of it. She felt very pleased with herself and wished Charlotte was with her to share the moment. She had never felt so happy and wanted to share it all with her best friend. But no matter how hard Hannah wished, it was Miles riding Toffee, not Charlotte.

Then, just as Hannah was bringing Flash back into a trot, she realised that she had been daydreaming. Hannah felt the saddle slip and tried to push her foot firmly down into the stirrup to bring it level again. But the saddle had slipped too far and one of the saddlebags was pulling against her. She was going to fall off!

Miles saw what was happening and quickly kicked Toffee forward. He rushed to Flash's head and brought the pony to a standstill. But the saddle still slipped right over and Hannah fell to the ground. She fell quite hard, but she was unhurt.

Frank pulled the canoe in, leaped out and raced over. Hannah lay on the ground wrestling with a saddlebag.

'I couldn't help it,' said Hannah, picking herself up. 'The saddle started slipping and I couldn't stop it.'

Frank examined the saddle.

'The girth's too loose,' he said. 'You didn't tighten it properly.'

Hannah lowered her head and studied her boots. She was feeling really miserable now. She couldn't believe how quickly her mood had changed.

'Never mind,' said Miles. 'Don't worry.' He put the saddle back in its proper place and tightened the girth securely.

Mum came over and gave Hannah a hug.

'You'll be all right now. I'll give you a leg-up,' she said.

'I think I'll lead him for a bit,' said Hannah. She was a little shaken.

Suddenly, Hannah had lost all her confidence.

The afternoon grew warm and overcast. Dark ragged rain-clouds gathered over the mountain. Hannah eventually climbed back up into the saddle but didn't attempt anything more than a gentle walk.

By the time they reached the second outpost the sky was almost as black as night.

'I think we're in for a real storm,' said Frank.

He pulled the canoe right out of the water and dragged it high up on to the bank.

By the time they had settled into the

cabin and Hannah and Miles had unsaddled the ponies and made them
comfortable in the outside shelter, the first
drops of rain had started to fall.

There was just about enough time to
gather firewood before the heavens
opened and the rain poured down in stair
rods.

The arrangement inside the log cabin
was the same as before, and Mum soon
had the kettle singing away on the gas
cooker.

Frank lit the woodburner and they sat
at the scrubbed table listening to the gentle patter of rain on the roof.

Hannah was worried about Flash being
outside in the storm, but Miles said that
he was a Welsh Mountain pony and
would be used to harsh weather.

Later, there was thunder, and sheet
lightning which lit up the cabin with
bright flashes.

Hannah didn't like the storm at all but
it felt safe, warm and cosy inside the

cabin. She kept going to the window and thinking about the two ponies outside. Frank lit the oil lamps and Mum cooked a meal of sausages and beans.

After supper, Hannah sneaked outside. She pulled her sweatshirt up over her head and made a dash for the shelter. Flash and Toffee seemed totally unmoved by the thunder and lightning. They lowered their heads and closed their eyes against the storm. Beneath the shelter both ponies were warm and dry. Hannah smiled to

herself and felt silly for worrying. She gave them a quick pat, then raced back inside.

As she lay in her bed with the lights out, the rain was still falling in torrents. Hannah fell asleep listening to the steady hammering of rain on the roof.

It rained all through the night and, although the following morning was clear and bright, the river was brimming to its banks, swollen from the heavy downpour.

As they took breakfast out on to the covered veranda, bits of debris, branches and driftwood floated past in a mad scramble through the water.

The river was no longer the calm, gentle waterway of the day before, but a fierce, powerful torrent with foaming waves crashing over rocks and tree roots.

Mum looked apprehensive about taking the canoe out but Frank said it would be all right.

'It just means less paddling,' he said, trying to bring comfort to the situation. 'And with this wind, we'll simply sail along.'

Hannah saddled up Flash. She checked the girth three times. Frank strapped the saddlebags in place and they were on their way.

Hannah's fall the day before had upset her more than she had realised. She was jumpy in the saddle, which unsettled Flash, and the pony twisted and shied at every turn and command.

Mum and Frank battled with the canoe to keep it on an even course, avoiding the storm debris, which kept drifting out into their path.

At one point they just narrowly missed a floating log and had to paddle like crazy to avoid it. They sailed away round a bend in the river at great speed. Miles was up ahead on Toffee and for a moment Hannah lost sight of everyone completely. Beginning to panic, she hurried Flash on until they caught up with Miles at the next bend.

They carried on steadily for another two hours before the accident happened.

# Five

Hannah and Flash were concentrating hard on getting down a particularly tricky slope, and it wasn't until they had got safely to the bottom that Hannah's eye was caught by a strange rock formation, just across the river. Two enormous boulders balanced on top of a third. They had been carved by the wind, over time, into what Hannah thought looked like a big white bear. She spotted the canoe coming down the river, and was just about to shout to Mum and Frank about the funny-shaped boulders, when a loud cracking noise made her snap her head round. The fierce storm the night before had really whipped the river up. The raging water had driven hard against the muddy banks and washed all the earth away from the tree roots. The wind had done the rest and left one tree leaning dangerously over the river. With a tremendous creak and a ripping of roots, Hannah saw the tree fall right before her eyes.

It plunged into the water, falling right across the path of the canoe. Hannah called out as a wild branch caught the front of the canoe and hit the fibreglass nose with a loud smack across its bow. The branch missed Hannah's mum, who was sitting at the front, but the force of the impact made her drop the paddle which, in turn, tipped the canoe over.

Hannah screamed as she saw Mum and Frank disappear beneath the foaming water. The tree rocked and rolled in the river, still held to the bank by a tangle of twisted roots. The canoe spun away and sailed down river, upside down.

Hannah threw herself out of the saddle and rushed to the bank. Miles was already there. Frank was the first to bob to the surface, his life-jacket forcing him up out of the water. His helmet floated alongside him. Somehow the strap had snapped under the pressure of water when the canoe had capsized.

Frank quickly grabbed hold of Mum and held her head above the water as he swam with her towards the bank.

Hannah reached out with Miles and helped pull her mother up the muddy bank. Hannah pulled with all her strength until Mum was lying on dry ground out of the river.

But the bank was really slippery and Frank lost his hold when he tried to climb out. Miles went to grab him, but Frank fell backwards, hitting his head on a rock.

Frank lay motionless, face down in the water. He drifted away, caught in the branches of the tree, three metres from the bank.

Hannah acted very quickly. As Mum struggled to her feet, Hannah began to crawl on all fours along the length of the tree trunk, using it as a bridge from the bank to where Frank lay. She snapped a loose branch free and hooked its end to

Frank's life-jacket. Miles followed behind Hannah. He saw straight away what she was trying to do.

As Mum lowered herself back into the water using the tree roots for support, Hannah and Miles pulled with all their strength and managed to float Frank away from the tangle of foliage. The life-jacket kept Frank buoyant and Hannah held him there in the main stream of the river as Mum and Miles reached out and caught hold of his trouser legs.

Between them they were able to haul Frank into the bank.

Mum quickly turned Frank over. Thankfully he was still breathing, but there was a nasty cut to the side of his head. His dark hair was plastered to his face with blood and water. But he was alive.

Hannah helped to pull Frank right up on to the bank. He was very heavy, but after a struggle they had him lying on his back, safely out of the water.

Then Hannah's mum broke down, sobbing like a baby.

'Frank,' she cried. 'Oh Frank. Wake up. Please wake up.'

'Dad!' yelled Miles. He sounded scared.

But Frank didn't move. He lay there with his eyes closed, his breathing shallow. The gash to his head was nasty and his face was covered in blood.

'We've got to get help,' sobbed Mum. 'Frank's badly hurt. Take Flash and Toffee and ride as quickly as you can to the next outpost. Bring help.'

'But what if there's no one there?' Hannah was crying too now, but trying to be brave for her mum's sake.

'Then you might have to ride back to base camp. Be as quick as you can, but please be careful. I'll have to stay here and look after Frank,' She gave Hannah a hug. 'You can do it. Both of you. I know you can.'

Miles's face had turned a ghostly white.

Flash stood on the bank watching. He

was becoming restless and stamping his hooves. All the activity and shouting had unsettled the little pony. Toffee had wandered a little way off but Miles caught him and quickly mounted.

Mum took the saddlebags off the ponies to make things easier. Hannah adjusted her riding hat, fixed the strap under her chin and climbed into the saddle. She was still nervous that the saddle might slip again. Mum checked the girth and squeezed Hannah's hand.

Poor Hannah was shaking with nerves.

'We'll be as quick as we can,' she said. Her voice was quavery as she fought back the tears.

'Do be careful,' said Mum. 'I love you.'

Hannah dug in her heels and set off down the mountain, following Miles towards the next outpost.

The going was steady. Hannah and Miles were able to canter along the easier parts of the bridle-path but had to pull the ponies up to a walk when the path zig-zagged close to the river.

Part of the time they were in woodlands. But the rest of the time they were out in the open valley on the mountain-side. The river raged fiercely as it tumbled along. Hannah's heart lurched when she saw the broken canoe beached on some rocks in the middle of the river. There was a big hole in its side and the bow was smashed to pieces.

Then the bridle-path took a steep turn leading downwards, and below her Hannah could see the outpost. Her spirits lifted and she prayed that someone would be there.

They rode down and jumped off the ponies, running with them to the log cabin. The door was locked. There was no one there.

Miles checked around the back but the place was deserted.

The sky had darkened again and the first spots of rain began to fall. Hannah mounted again quickly. If there was no one at the next outpost they decided they would ride all the way to base camp. The rain urged them on.

Hannah kicked Flash into a trot. Toffee had a longer stride and it was all Hannah could do to keep up. The rain had brought with it a bitter wind. Hannah felt chilled to the bone but she gritted her teeth and rode on.

The next outpost was also deserted. Hannah was worried to death about Mum and Frank. So was Miles. Please let them be OK, she prayed, as they set off for base camp.

The fine, misty drizzle made it difficult to see far ahead, and the bridle-path became steep and slippery in parts. But Flash was brilliant and Hannah rode bravely on. They had to get help. They were the ones Mum and Frank were depending on.

Suddenly Flash stopped. Hannah felt herself lurch forward in the saddle but she pushed her seat down and stayed on.

Flash had stopped because Toffee had suddenly stumbled in front of him, and Miles had fallen awkwardly from the saddle.

He picked himself up and held his wrist. 'Oh, no!' he groaned, nursing his hand. He winced with pain. 'I think I've sprained it.'

Miles bent down and examined Toffee's hoof.

'Poor Toffee's had it too. He's lost a shoe and gone lame. There's nothing for it, Hannah – I'm sorry, but you'll have to go on alone.'

Hannah's tummy wobbled and slid into her boots.

The storm had brought down a large branch from the overhead canopy of trees and it was completely blocking their path.

Hannah studied the barricade then desperately looked at Miles. A steep bank rose to the right with the river rushing by on her left. There was no other way through but over.

'I'll walk Toffee back,' said Miles. 'You can make it, Hannah. I know you can.'

Hannah leaned forward and patted her pony's thick neck.

She took a deep breath and gathered her thoughts.

'Go on, Hannah. It's not very high. You can take it!' Miles had no idea that Hannah wasn't very good at jumping.

They backed up. Hannah gave Miles a weak smile, then urged Flash forward. She closed her eyes and tried to picture Charlotte in her mind. It was like watching a video in slow motion with Charlotte taking a pony over a row of barrels. Then suddenly everything fell into place and Flash flew like a bird over the jump. Without looking back they thundered on.

Hannah passed the last two outposts without even glancing sideways. It seemed pointless somehow. If help was to be found it would be at base camp. Hannah was certain of this now.

She urged Flash to keep going. The rain had stopped but the cold wind stung her cheeks and made her eyes stream. Her clothes were soaked right through.

Hannah took a steep path, remembering to lean back in the saddle to help Flash keep his footing. Then they were on the flat and she found herself shouting, shouting for Flash to go faster, FASTER!

# Six

At last, the base camp came into view. Hannah could see the lodge in the distance and the ranger's Land Rover parked outside. But her heart sank as she saw the ranger climb into the vehicle and drive off.

'No!' yelled Hannah. Her voice echoed painfully across the mountain pass. 'Come back. Please come back!'

Hannah pulled Flash up and stood in the stirrups, shouting and waving. But the Land Rover showed no sign of stopping. It disappeared down a track and was gone.

Hannah galloped on. The bridle-path was flat and became much wider as it left the river and stretched down past the lodge, joining the track which the ranger had taken. Hannah thought if she carried on, she might be able to catch him up. She didn't know where the ranger was going but he was her only hope. Unless there was someone else at the camp! A new hope flickered into life.

Hannah stopped at the lodge. She leaped out of the saddle and hammered on the door with her fist, willing it to open. 'Please answer. Please answer,' she whispered to herself. Hannah waited and waited but no one came. And as her hand fell away from the door she suddenly felt very cold, tired and frightened.

She burst into tears, her body racked

with sobs. 'There must be *someone*,' she cried. 'But where?'

Flash nudged her gently with his muzzle and gave a low whicker. He seemed to be urging Hannah to carry on. Hannah clutched the reins in one hand and pulled herself back into the saddle.

'Thanks, Flash,' she whispered. She leaned forward and gave the little pony a hug.

Then Hannah squeezed with her heels and gently kicked Flash into action. She had to keep trying. She had to get help for Frank. She was the only one who could do it.

Hannah rode along the same track the ranger had taken. The road was pitted with holes and Hannah slowed Flash to a gentle trot. It was too dangerous to go any faster. She didn't want Flash going lame too!

Up ahead, Hannah caught sight of a small, stone cottage, nestling back off the road. The cottage was almost hidden from view by a huge tree which bent low over its grey slate roof. The tree's branches hugged the dwelling in a protective embrace.

Hannah jumped off Flash and ran with him up the sidepath. She hammered on the door, calling for help. Hannah pressed her ear to the wooden panel. She could hear movement inside. Someone was in there – why weren't they opening the door?

'*Please* open up.' Hannah rapped on the door again. 'I *know* there's someone there. I can hear you. Please open the door. It's an emergency!'

The door creaked and swung inwards slowly. A young girl of about seven stood there. A long dark passage stretched behind her.

'Can you fetch your mum or dad?' Hannah said. 'Please! I need their help.'

The little girl looked up at Hannah with big brown eyes. 'There's no one here,' she said. 'They've gone to help at the bridge.'

'The bridge?' said Hannah, puzzled.

'The river has flooded and the bridge is down,' said the girl. 'They're all at the bridge.'

Hannah was about to ask how far down river the bridge was, but the girl looked frightened and closed the door.

The bridge. Hannah had to get to the bridge. With new hope and confidence she swung into the saddle. Suddenly it was as if she had been riding all her life. Hannah turned Flash and galloped away down river.

However far it was, she would make it. Hannah was sure of that now. She was going to find help.

At last the bridge came into sight. There were at least half a dozen men down there, heaving and humping large rocks and boulders as they worked to rebuild the stone crossing. The river had swept part of the bridge away and the men fought against the fierce current to save the remaining structure.

Hannah felt dizzy and very tired. She had been in the saddle for over two hours.

The men looked up as Hannah pulled Flash to an abrupt halt at the nearside bank. The ranger recognised Hannah straight away and came over as she leaped from the saddle, yelling above the roar of the river.

'Help,' she called. 'Please help me!'

Seeing the ranger and the men made Hannah's face crumple. She told of the accident up river, and how Frank was badly hurt. How she and Miles had left Mum looking after him. And how Miles had been forced to turn back on Toffee.

The ranger took off his coat and slipped it around Hannah's shoulders. She couldn't stop herself from shivering. A woman appeared, put a comforting arm around Hannah and led her to the ranger's Land Rover.

'There,' she said. 'You'll be warmer inside.' Hannah smiled and nodded. But first she wanted to make sure that Flash was all right after his long ride. Flash was a hero and Hannah didn't just want to leave him and go off. She gave the pony a big hug and stroked his face. Flash pushed his soft velvet muzzle into Hannah's hand and blew hot breaths into her palm. The ranger assured Hannah that Flash would be taken care of. His lad was coming over from the stables and Flash would be rubbed down and watered straight away.

Hannah said goodbye to Flash and settled into the back seat, pulling the coat around her. The ranger's wife climbed into the driver's seat and switched on the heater.

'You'd best come with me and we'll get you out of those wet clothes,' she said.

The ranger opened the passenger door, jumped in and flicked on the two-way radio. As his wife drove towards their cottage, he was busy speaking to Mountain Rescue and raising an alert, giving details of the accident and the location up river.

Hannah breathed a sigh of relief. Now that the rescue no longer depended on her alone, she began to relax a little. She hadn't realised how tired she was after the long rescue ride.

'You're a real heroine, do you know that?' said the ranger.

But all Hannah could think about was Mum, Frank and Miles.

# Seven

As Hannah clambered out of the Land Rover and followed the ranger and his wife into the cottage, she heard a tremendous noise overhead. A loud droning sound. She looked up to the sky and saw a yellow rescue helicopter whirring above them on its way up the mountain.

'Don't you worry about a thing, my

dear,' said the ranger's wife. She was full of concern. 'Mountain Rescue will be there in the blink of an eye. We'll get you into some dry clothes and then drive you to the hospital. Your mother and everyone will probably be there before we arrive.'

Hannah changed out of her wet clothes and into some nice dry ones. The ranger had a daughter about the same age as Hannah, and the clothes – jeans and a big thick sweater – fitted perfectly. Hannah sat by the open kitchen range warming herself and sipping hot steaming tea from a big mug.

Then a message come through on the ranger's radio which almost made Hannah's heart stop.

Mountain Rescue couldn't find Mum and Frank. They had circled the area and found nothing. Not a sign.

The ranger passed the handset to Hannah. Mountain Rescue needed Hannah to describe the river in more detail so they could find the exact spot where the accident happened.

'Was there anything different about that stretch of the river, Hannah? *Over.*'

Hannah could hardly breathe.

'No. It all looked the same,' said Hannah.

'Are you sure, Hannah? Think carefully. *Over!*'

'There was a bend. I think.' Poor Hannah's mind was racing. 'Lots of trees . . .' her voice trailed off. Then she remembered. 'YES! And boulders! Three enormous white boulders in the shape of a giant bear – there on the opposite bank.'

'Bear Rock. Got it, Hannah. *Over and out.*'

The ranger kept in constant radio contact with Mountain Rescue and reported to Hannah that Mum, Frank and Miles had been found and lifted safely off the mountain. A horse box was also on its way to collect poor Toffee.

Frank was fine and, apart from a nasty

bump on his head, he was going to be all right. He had regained consciousness and was feeling well enough to send a message to Hannah not to worry and that he and Mum would see her at the hospital.

It was a half-hour drive to the hospital and, as the ranger's wife drove the Land Rover, Hannah fell asleep in the back. She was absolutely exhausted.

Mum was sitting with Frank and Miles in Casualty when Hannah arrived. Frank had already been seen by a doctor and was sporting a white bandage around his head. Hannah couldn't help thinking how much it made him look like a proper Frankenstein's monster. But she preferred not to see him like that any more – instead, she decided that he looked like a handsome tennis player in a sweatband.

As usual, Miles was scribbling away in his notebook. His injured wrist was wrapped in a bandage but nothing was going to stop him writing down the details of their exciting rescue. He looked up and gave Hannah a big smile. 'Well done, Hannah. I knew you could do it!'

Hannah threw herself into Mum's arms and Frank gave the two of them a big hug.

'I didn't know if I was ever going to see you again,' sobbed Hannah.

Mum brushed the hair from Hannah's eyes.

'It'll take more than a bump on the head to keep me from seeing you,' said Frank.

Hannah was so happy that they were all safe and sound. She couldn't believe how pleased she was that they were together again. It was like they were a real family.

Frank's car had been driven to the hospital along with all their belongings, and they decided to spend the remaining days in a hotel.

'No point in cutting the holiday short,' said Frank. 'And it will be good for all of us to rest up for a day or two.'

Miles told Hannah that he was writing a report about the rescue in his notebook. And he wanted a detailed account from Hannah about everything that had happened. A proper interview. He was going to send the article to the local newspaper when they got home. Hannah blushed with pride. It was going to be all about *her*.

The Portmeirion Hotel made a pleasant change from the outdoor arrangements of the Llanstwyth Adventure Park. There was a swimming pool and plenty to do in the daytime. They took long walks in the countryside, played pitch-and-putt on the crazy-golf course, and enjoyed being lazy for a day or two.

Mum drove the car on the way home as Frank's head was still a little sore. Frank sat in the back with Hannah and listened carefully for the umpteenth time as she told him every detail of her amazing adventure, riding down the mountain on Flash.

'We're lucky we had such a good rescue rider,' said Mum. 'I'm really proud of you, Hannah.'

'And Flash was brilliant,' said Hannah. 'I'm going to miss him.'

Hannah thought back to jumping the fallen tree on Flash. It had felt so natural, and she'd been in such a hurry that she'd almost completely forgotten about her nerves. Now, at last, Hannah felt that she could really ride. She couldn't wait to get back and tell Charlotte all about it. Then she remembered saying goodbye to Flash and felt a lump the size of a grapefruit in her throat. Hannah closed her eyes and imagined hugging the pony and planting that last kiss on his velvet nose. 'Goodbye Flash,' she whispered to herself, 'and thank you.'

On the first Saturday after they arrived home, it was Hannah's birthday. Through the letterbox came heaps of cards. Inside some of them were letters and money from aunts and uncles with messages that said 'buy yourself a little something' or 'buy a present of your choice'. Hannah stood all the cards in a line on the mantelpiece then put all the birthday money into one of the envelopes. She knew exactly what she was going to do with it. The money was going straight into her pony fund.

Hannah opened her presents. There was a package from Charlotte which her mother had dropped in the day before. Inside was a T-shirt with a brown horse galloping across the front of it. Hannah held it up against herself and gave Mum and Frank a big smile. It was great.

Miles was still away at school, but he had sent Hannah his newspaper article inside a card. The local paper had printed the story on their front page. Hannah beamed when she read it. It was Miles's very first newspaper article. Hannah was so pleased for him.

Then Hannah opened the huge cardboard box that Frank had placed on the table. She tore open the wrapping paper excitedly. Inside the box was a pair of riding jodhpurs, a hacking jacket and a shiny pair of brand-new riding boots.

'Wow!' said Hannah. 'Thank you.' She leaped up and gave Mum and Frank each a big hug and a kiss.

Hannah could hardly wait to try her new riding clothes on.

'They're just perfect,' she said. 'Brill. Can I wear them when I go riding with Charlotte this afternoon?'

'Of course you can,' laughed Mum. 'That's what they're for!'

Hannah raced upstairs to get changed. She wanted to put on her new riding clothes straight away. And she was so excited with her presents that she didn't notice the secret looks that Mum and Frank exchanged. Mum was beaming and Frank gave a little special wink.

Charlotte's father picked Hannah up in the car as usual and drove the two girls to the riding stables.

'Happy Birthday, Han,' smiled Charlotte. She admired Hannah's new riding outfit. 'You look great. Did your Mum and Frankenstein buy you that lot?'

Hannah nodded. 'But his name's Frank, not Frankenstein.' She pulled at the sleeve of her new jacket. 'I don't call him that any more!'

'You'll be calling him Dad soon, I expect,' joked Charlotte.

'I hope so.' Hannah felt herself blush. 'He's really nice.'

'You've changed your tune,' said Charlotte.

On the way, Hannah quickly told Charlotte all about the holiday. Charlotte's mouth dropped open when she heard about Hannah's rescue ride on Flash. She hadn't seen the newspaper article yet and wanted to hear every detail.

'Wow, that must have been fantastic,' said Charlotte. 'You're full of surprises, aren't you!'

When they arrived at the stables Mrs Bellows came out from the stalls. Hannah and Charlotte were the first to arrive.

'My, my,' said Mrs Bellows as she eyed Hannah up and down. 'You look like a proper little rider. And I don't expect you'll be wanting to ride Bracken any more, from what I've heard,' she added.

Hannah looked puzzled. Just what exactly *had* she heard, wondered Hannah. She secretly hoped that Mrs Bellows had read Miles's newspaper article.

'So I've got a very special pony waiting for you inside instead,' Mrs Bellows continued.

Hannah followed her into the stable. She got quite a shock inside. Mum and Frank were standing there, grinning; and behind them, in saddle and bridle, was a beautiful golden palomino. The pony of Hannah's dreams.

'His name is Golden Fern,' smiled Mum.

'Happy birthday, Hannah,' said Frank. 'He's all yours. A very special present for a very brave girl. At last, a pony of your very own.'

Charlotte was speechless. And all Hannah could do was stand there with her mouth open, staring wide-eyed at the beautiful golden pony.

She threw herself at her mum, wrapping her arms around her waist.

'Oh, Mum,' cried Hannah. 'Is he really mine? He's just perfect.'

'He's all yours,' said Frank, ruffling her hair. 'Forever and ever.'

Hannah couldn't thank them both enough. A pony all of her own. She could hardly believe it. She had never had such a wonderful present in all her life.

Hannah looked around at all the smiling faces then stepped towards the pony. His muzzle felt as soft as velvet. And, as Hannah snuggled into his neck, the palomino whickered softly and pushed his head against her. Hannah shivered with excitement. She couldn't wait to ride him. And she knew right there and then that she and Golden Fern were going to be the very best of friends. Always.

If you enjoyed this **Rescue Riders** story
look out for book two, *Fire Alert*.

Here's an extract
to whet your appetite!

# One

'Some days,' said Hannah, 'I wonder if all this is worth it!' She looked across at her best friend, Charlotte, who nodded in agreement and reined in her pony, Mandrake. Today was turning into exactly one of those days.

Sitting on their ponies in the middle of the windswept downs, the two girls

1

hunched their shoulders and turned up their collars against the drizzling rain. They had been practising for next week's riding competition for the last hour and it hadn't stopped raining the whole time. Hannah for one was more than ready to turn her back on the whole thing and trek home on Flash, her golden palomino. The pony's real name was Golden Fern, but Flash was his special nickname – after the pony that had really taught Hannah how to ride. She breathed down her gloves to warm her frozen fingers, patted Flash's neck and wished that the practice would come to an end.

'Come on, you two over there. For goodness sake, wake up!' Mrs Bellows, their riding schoolteacher, was standing up in her stirrups and yelling in their direction at the top of her voice.

Hannah and Charlotte suddenly realised that the B team had finished their flag race – dashing down a course planting flags in waiting buckets – and their own team was about to start practising for the old sock race – much like a relay race but using an old rolled-up sock.

'Hey, Charlotte. Old Bellows is in a real mood today,' murmured Hannah as she urged Flash into position at the top of the line.

'And so would you be if you had such a feeble lot to deal with,' snapped Mrs Bellows sharply from behind her.

'Oops!' Charlotte pulled a face at Hannah.

'Don't you *ever* want to beat the Craxley team?' Mrs Bellows was looking straight at them.

Of course we do, thought Hannah. Why do you think we're here? But she didn't dare say it. Not out loud anyway.

'I suppose she thinks we're here waiting for Santa Claus,' whispered Charlotte. She always seemed to know just what Hannah was thinking. But she was careful to turn her head as she spoke just in case Mrs Bellows could lip-read.

They had been practising for their races for months, and now, with the area competition just two weeks away, Mrs Bellows had them all up on the downs for an hour every day after school perfecting their techniques.

Hannah squeezed Flash with her calves and the golden palomino pranced forward. He really was a beautiful horse – golden blonde, just like Hannah. Eager to please, he danced on the spot next to Charlotte and Mandrake. Mandrake was fourteen hands and jet-black. You couldn't find a blacker pony if you tried. Charlotte, with her dark bob and striking features, made a perfect partner for him.

Mandrake pawed at the ground and tossed his head, eager to stretch out and race. Mandrake was very fast. The fastest pony in the team.

'It wouldn't be so bad if she didn't shout at us all the time,' said Hannah. 'It's not as if we don't listen or know what to do!'

At the front of the line, Mrs Bellows waved her right arm high in the air, like a general about to charge into battle. The first rider streaked down the opening run.

'Prepare yourself, Charlotte. Ready. Go!'

'See you, Han.' Charlotte urged Mandrake forward and leaned out to receive the rolled-up sock from the incoming rider's outstretched hand. Then she loosened her reins slightly and kicked Mandrake hard. The pony lurched forward and shot away like a bullet.

'You're supposed to squeeze gently with your legs! You're not supposed to kick!' Hannah shouted after her. But her voice was already lost in the grey drizzle.

Now it was Hannah's turn. She pressed her seat down in the saddle as Sophie Warren loomed up on Pickles. But, as Hannah leaned forward, a flurry of raindrops hit Flash in the face and he backed up suddenly just as Hannah reached out. The sock slipped from Hannah's fingers and rolled on to the ground.

Quick as lightning, Sophie leaped from Pickles, retrieved the sock and handed it up to Hannah. Then Flash was away.

'Come on, boy,' yelled Hannah. Flash's creamy-white mane sailed out in the wind. He was going as fast as he knew how. Without Hannah needing to check Flash's stride, they reached the home bucket.

Hannah held on to Flash with her legs, bent low across his shoulder and dropped the sock into the container. But the drizzle made her misjudge and the sock caught the rim of the bucket and bounced out.

'Nice one, Han!' It was Charlotte. Hannah could have killed her.

'Well, that was awful,' said Mrs Bellows. 'Come on, we'll do it again. And again. And again. Until we get it right.'

The rain had eased up now, but that made little difference to the A team's performance. In fact it became worse. This time *everything* went wrong. Riders fumbled with changeovers, ponies kicked the home bucket. And Hannah somehow managed to lose the sock completely. It flew out of her hand at one point and just seemed to disappear into thin air.

'There's not much point in entering at all if you're going to be as bad as this,' said Mrs Bellows. Hannah opened her mouth to speak.

'And it's no use complaining about the weather, either. It could be even worse on the day,' said Mrs Bellows.

Hannah's jaw hung open catching stray raindrops.

'Right then. You lot with your own ponies, same time tomorrow. My lot . . . home! Follow me. Trot ON,' she hollered. 'UP down. UP down. UP down.'

Hannah and Charlotte were the only two with their own ponies and used to being out on their own. They watched as the trail of riding-school ponies set off across the downs.

'Don't let her get to you, Han,' said Charlotte as they began to hack home in the opposite direction. It would only take them about twenty minutes along the main road once off the downs.

'It's all right for you,' said Hannah. 'You never do anything wrong.'

'That's because I'm a brill rider,' joked Charlotte. 'Race you to Tombstones.' Then she kicked Mandrake into a gallop.

'You're not supposed to . . .' began

Hannah, but Charlotte was already streaking away.

'Wait for me!'

If you enjoyed this **Rescue Riders** story
look out for book three, *Ghost Pony*.

Here's an extract
to whet your appetite!

# One

'Something's definitely going on!' said
Hannah.

Charlotte looked puzzled, and blinked
hard beneath a quizzical frown.

'What is? What's definitely going on?'
She tried to sound interested but was
actually more concerned with getting
Mandrake's bridle on before he started

1

playing up. If Charlotte didn't slip the bit behind Mandrake's teeth at exactly the right moment he would go on strike and clamp his jaws tight. And when Mandrake did that, you needed a crowbar to get the snaffle in. Or at least a peppermint!

'YES!' Charlotte exclaimed in triumph as Mandrake took the bit. She turned her attention back to Hannah, who had long since finished tacking up Flash and was now busy with other thoughts.

'So *what's* definitely going on?' asked Charlotte again.

'It's Miles,' said Hannah. She reached forward to smooth out Flash's creamy mane and give him a good rub behind his ears. Flash was a golden palomino whose coat shone like shot silk in the early morning sunlight. 'Miles is definitely up to something!'

Miles was Hannah's stepbrother. He was sixteen and dead keen to be a newspaper journalist when he left school. He now had a Saturday job, helping out at the offices of the local paper. And he'd already managed to get two small news reports printed. Both pieces had been about Hannah. The first was an account of her heroic rescue ride down a Welsh mountain after an accident on an adventure holiday. And the second was about Hannah and her friends saving the old mill on the downs from burning to the ground.

Miles was always on the lookout for a good scoop. He was always in the

3

background somewhere, snooping about like a shadow.

Hannah explained. 'I've noticed that Miles has been leaving the house really early for the last four days. Much earlier than usual. He always leaves before seven anyway for his newspaper round. But since Monday he's been slipping out before six.'

'How do you know?' said Charlotte. 'And why are you awake at that time, anyway?'

'It's the gravel,' said Hannah. 'Those fat tyres on his new mountain bike make a real noise on the drive. And it's right below my bedroom window, so I hear him crunching past as he leaves. Yes! Miles is definitely up to something!'

'I bet it's that ghost pony,' said Charlotte, matter-of-factly. Then she checked Mandrake's girth.

'Ghost pony! *What* ghost pony?' Hannah couldn't believe her ears. She knew nothing about any ghost pony and was

4

surprised that Charlotte did and hadn't told her.

Charlotte pushed her dark hair back off her forehead and crammed her riding hat down on to her head.

'You know,' she said casually. 'The ghost pony. I'm sure I told you. Or someone else must have.'

'You didn't tell me about any ghost pony,' complained Hannah. 'No one did. I can't believe *you* didn't tell me either. I'm probably the last person in the whole universe to know about it! How could you not tell me?'

'Keep your hair on,' teased Charlotte. 'It's no big deal.' She suddenly felt really embarrassed that she had forgotten to tell her best friend about it. 'It's only a story that's going round, Han.'

'And who told you?'

'I overheard my mum on the phone telling her friend about a strange white pony which has been spotted up on the moors. Only a few people have seen it,' continued Charlotte, 'but they all report the same thing. A thin, ghostly pale pony which suddenly appears from nowhere, then disappears back into the mist again before anyone can get a really close look.'

'Wow!' breathed Hannah. 'That's fantastic! And I bet that's exactly what big bruvver Milo is up to. He's out on that moor looking for this phantom pony so that he can write about it for the paper. I can see it now: GHOST PONY HAUNTS MOOR!'

'You'd make a great detective, Han,' laughed Charlotte. 'Sharp as a razor, you are.'

Hannah pulled a face. 'If you're so clever, then tell me why Miles hasn't said anything? Why is he being so secretive? I would have thought that I was the first person he would have confided in.'

'I can't believe you've said that, Han. It's quite obvious. Miles knows exactly what you're like. You'd be begging to tag along. You know you would. You'd cramp his style and spoil it for him.'

'No, I wouldn't!' complained Hannah bitterly. Then, 'Yes, I would,' she admitted honestly. 'But wait till I catch up with him anyway. I shan't beg to go along with him. But I *shall* pester him until he tells me everything he knows about it!'

Charlotte swung herself up into the saddle and laughed. 'Something tells me I'm going to be up on that moor really early tomorrow morning.'

'Earlier than you think!' grinned Hannah.

# RESCUE RIDERS
## *Peter Clover*

| 0 340 72679 2 | Race Against Time | £3.50 ☐ |
| 0 340 72680 6 | Fire Alert | £3.50 ☐ |
| 0 340 72681 4 | Ghost Pony | £3.50 ☐ |

*All Hodder Children's books are available at your local bookshop or newsagent, or can be ordered direct from the publisher. Just tick the titles you want and fill in the form below. Prices and availability subject to change without notice.*

Hodder Children's Books, Cash Sales Department, Bookpoint, 39 Milton Park, Abingdon, OXON, OX14 4TD, UK. If you have a credit card you may order by telephone – (01253) 400414.

Please enclose a cheque or postal order made payable to Bookpoint Ltd to the value of the cover price and allow the following for postage and packing:
UK & BFPO – £1.00 for the first book, 50p for the second book, and 30p for each additional book ordered up to a maximum charge of £3.00.
OVERSEAS & EIRE – £2.00 for the first book, £1.00 for the second book, and 50p for each additional book.

Name ...................................................................................
........................................................................................
Address................................................................................
........................................................................................

If you would prefer to pay by credit card, please complete:
Please debit my Visa/Access/Diner's Card/American Express (delete as applicable) card no:

| | | | | | | | | | | | | | | | | | | |
|---|---|---|---|---|---|---|---|---|---|---|---|---|---|---|---|---|---|---|

Signature ............................................................................
Expiry Date.........................................................................